S0-ARO-000

The Heebie Jeebie

by Lisa Thompson
illustrated by Mike Golding

sundance™

Characters

Toby

Olivia

Lurk

Spook

2

Contents

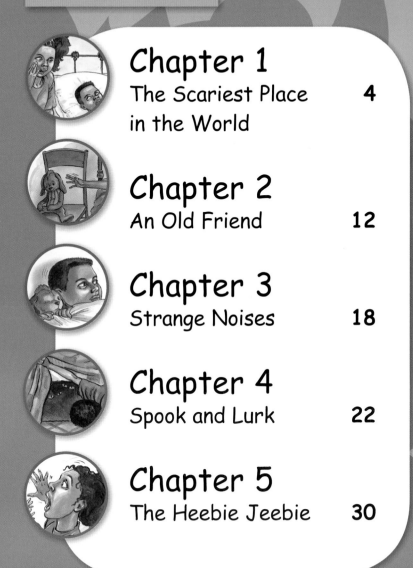

Chapter 1

The Scariest Place in the World

"Toby, are you sure you'll be all right sleeping out here?" asked Grandma as she tucked him into the big bed in the back room. "Wouldn't you be more comfortable in the room you normally sleep in when you stay over?"

"Oh, don't worry, Gran," said Toby's sister Olivia, who was sitting on a chair next to the bed, "Toby won't be sleeping here all night. Just keep the hallway light on so he can make his way back to the other room." She lowered her voice so only Toby could hear, "If they give you the chance."

Toby did his best to ignore his sister's comment. "I'll be fine, Gran," he said smiling, sounding as casual as he could.

Toby didn't want Gran to know he was scared out of his wits to be sleeping there. He didn't think she would be happy if she found out that the only reason he was sleeping in the back room was because Olivia had dared him to. Olivia said strange and scary things appeared there at night. She said she often saw them on her visits.

Gran gave Toby a kiss goodnight before she left. "Remember, I'm just down the hall if you need me," she said.

Knowing this did not make Toby feel one bit safer. Toby knew it wouldn't matter if she was down the hall or across town because Gran could sleep through a hurricane. Once asleep, there was no way Gran would hear his cries for help, if or when he made any.

"Just remember, they can smell your fear," said Olivia when Gran had gone. "And whatever you do, don't scream. It only gets them more excited."

"Will you stop trying to freak me out!" cried Toby.

"I'm just trying to be helpful," said Olivia, not very convincingly. "Try to go to sleep before they arrive. With a bit of luck they won't wake you and will leave you alone." She got up to leave. "I'll see you in the morning . . . hopefully."

"You bet," Toby answered cheerily. "You can make me breakfast while I tell you all about my dreams. I think I'll have eggs and bacon on toast, with some mushrooms on the side thanks."

As Olivia headed out of the room she flipped off the room and hallway lights, leaving Toby in total darkness. Suddenly Toby felt a wave of fear. He struggled to breathe. He tried to scream but no sound came. Then the hallway light flipped back on.

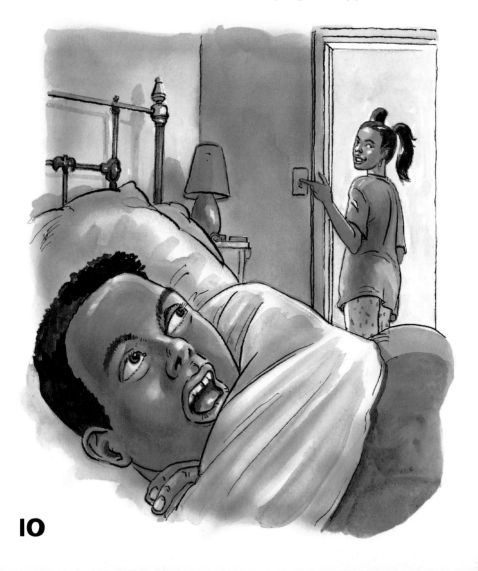

"Oops. Sorry about that," Olivia giggled from the other end of the hall. "I forgot how afraid you are of the dark. But then, that's nothing compared to the Jeepers Creepers. Goodnight little brother." Olivia was still giggling as she closed her bedroom door.

Toby was now all alone, waiting.

Chapter 2

An Old Friend

On his own in the back room, Toby felt like he was a million miles away from the rest of the house. He'd never slept in such a big room before, or such a big bed.

He looked toward the doorway and focused on the dim light coming in from the hall.

The light turned everything in the room into large shapes: a soaring rectangle for the chest of drawers, a looming square for the TV, a towering triangle for Gran's flower vase.

Gran had tucked him in so tightly he had to wriggle to get his arms free and turn his body. To the side of the bed, on the chair Olivia had been sitting in, he noticed a shape he hadn't seen in a long time.

It was Batbat, the teddy Gran had made for him
when he was little. Batbat was no ordinary teddy.
For a start he didn't look anything like a bear. He
had long limbs and big paws. His body was thin
and striped. His ears were floppy like a rabbit's,
and he had a face like a bat's.

Toby stretched his arm out as far as he could without having to get out of bed. He grabbed Batbat and brought him in under the covers.

Toby noticed that Batbat was looking even stranger than the last time he had seen him. He had lost an eye, and some of his bright orange stuffing was coming out of the back of his head, making it look like he was sporting a mohawk.

Despite Batbat's worn and torn state, Toby couldn't have been more pleased to see his old friend. With Batbat by his side, he didn't feel so alone. He settled in and tried to wish himself to sleep.

It was no good. All his senses were on high alert. Toby's ears told him how super-quiet the room was. He could feel the cold air of the room on his cheeks. He pulled the covers over his and Batbat's heads, leaving only a tiny peephole.

Toby noticed the sheets smelled like lavender and mothballs. He hoped the sweet smell could calm his fears. The back room felt like the scariest place in the whole world. He closed his eyes and hoped the Jeepers Creepers that Olivia spent hours telling him about didn't show up.

Then he heard a noise, a noise that made him stiffen with fright.

Chapter 3

Strange Noises

The scratching sound came from behind the curtains. Toby began to tremble. He held Batbat close and wrapped himself as tightly as he could in the smell of lavender and mothballs.

His ears picked up another sound. It was like something scraping across the ceiling. Toby peeked over the covers. His eyes darted around the room searching for what had made the sound.

Suddenly he saw something race across the ceiling. It moved too quickly for him to get a really good look. He was almost positive that it was a round shadow. But a shadow of what?

He lay statue still under the covers, too scared to move. Olivia had told him that *Jeepers Creepers* were sneaky. He figured they must be crawling into the dark corners and hiding in the cracks, waiting for the right moment to . . .

Suddenly there was a fast pitter-patter across the floor. It stopped under the bed. Toby heard what he thought was hissing. As he listened harder, it sounded more like wheezing. He definitely heard scratching and scraping.

Without any warning, Toby did the bravest—or silliest—thing he had ever done. He leaped out of bed, switched on the light, and stood in the middle of the room.

Shivers of fear were running up his spine. Toby did his best to appear brave and waited for whatever was under the bed to show itself.

After what felt like an eternity, a very deep voice from under the bed asked, "Where is the Heebie Jeebie?"

Chapter 4

Spook and Lurk

Toby's heart was beating as if he had run a marathon. Ever so slowly, he crouched down and peered under the bed.

In the furthest and darkest corner, he could just make out two small, round figures with wide, green eyes. They were getting closer and closer. Their long, clawed feet scraped and scratched the floor as they walked. Finally the little round figures made it into the light.

"Boo!" said the slightly bigger one.

Toby jumped back with fright. He was too scared to scream or make even the slightest noise.

The smaller creature let out a wheeze like a laugh.

"Ah, gets them every time," said the bigger one. He held up one of his six hands to Toby. "Relax. There is no need to be afraid." He smiled, revealing two rows of razor sharp teeth.

23

"My name is Spook, and this," he pointed with another hand to his companion, "is Lurk. What's your name?"

Toby opened his mouth to speak but nothing came out. He tried again, opening and closing his mouth like a fish. Finally, he managed to squeak, "Toby. My . . . my . . . my name is Toby. Are you J-J-J-Jeepers C-C-Creepers?"

"Hardly!" snorted Spook, sounding offended. Another of his hands reached up and switched off the light. "We prefer the dark."

Lurk puffed out his chest. "Do we look like a pair of scared beasties to you?"

"I . . . I . . . I don't know," stammered Toby. "You're the first night beasties I've ever seen."

"We are far braver night beasties than Jeepers Creepers!" Spook informed him. "We are part of the Night Beastie Security Patrol." He pointed to a tattoo on one of his six upper arms that read N.B.S.P. "It's our job to keep the night safe for the Jeepers Creepers. If it's safe, they can come in and scare the likes of you!"

"And it appears," added Lurk, "that this house has a scaring ban on it due to a Heebie Jeebie sighting."

"What is a Heebie Jeebie?" asked Toby, afraid of the answer.

"It's an unknown monstrous beastie," explained Spook.

"EXTREMELY dangerous!" added Lurk.

"So, have you seen anything suspicious lately?" asked Spook as he scanned the room. "Any kinds of sounds that have really made the hairs on the back of your neck stand up?"

"Only the ones you made," said Toby. "Maybe you could ask my sister if she's noticed anything. She says she's seen lots of night beasties."

"Great!" cried Spook so loudly that it made Toby jump. "Where can I spook, I mean, find her?"

"Down the hall. First door on the left," answered Toby.

"I'll lurk, I mean, search around while you question the sister," said Lurk, disappearing into the shadows.

Toby followed Spook up the hallway to Olivia's room.

Chapter 5

The Heebie Jeebie

"Boo!" said Spook with a razor-like grin.

Olivia almost leaped through the ceiling. Spook held out one of his hands. Olivia sank under her bedcovers and started shaking. Toby had never seen her go so pale, or her eyes open so wide. She pulled the covers up tightly so that only her head appeared over the edge.

"What . . . what . . . what are you?" Olivia was trembling so much she could hardly get her words out.

"His name is Spook. He's part of the Night Beastie Security Patrol," said Toby, pointing to Spook's tattoo. That only made Olivia's eyes open wider, and her face go paler. "There's been a report from a Jeepers Creeper about an unknown monstrous beastie, otherwise known as a Heebie Jeebie, in the house. Can you believe that, Olivia?" Olivia curled deeper into her covers.

"I was wondering if you had seen or heard anything that might help us find it," said Spook.

Olivia began muttering as she shook. Spook had to lean in close to hear what she was saying.

"This can't . . . be . . . real. Not real. They are just stories . . . stories I made up . . . to scare Toby. Not happening . . . just stories . . . no such things as Jeepers Creepers . . . not real."

Suddenly, Lurk yelled from the back room "Come quickly! I've netted the Heebie Jeebie!"

Spook raced down the hall, followed by Toby. They saw Lurk struggling with a large net.

"Be very careful!" cried Spook. "Who knows how dangerous and ferocious it is. Have you sprayed him with the Unknown Monstrous Beastie Relaxing Spray?"

"I have," wheezed Lurk rather slowly, letting go of the net so that a leg stuck out.

"Hey! That's not a Heebie Jeebie!" cried Toby, recognizing the leg instantly. He rushed forward and grabbed the net from Lurk. "This is Batbat." Toby freed Batbat from the net and held him up.

Lurk and Spook ducked for cover. "Look out! He's going to attack!" cried Spook, his voice quivering.

"No he won't," said Toby. "Batbat might look scary, but he wouldn't hurt a fly. He can't. He's a stuffed toy. My grandma made him for me when I was little."

Spook crawled out from where he had taken cover. He took a close look at Batbat and confirmed he was indeed stuffed. "It does appear our Heebie Jeebie situation has been resolved Lurk. Lurk? Lurk, where are you?"

Lurk was curled up among a pile of pillows. "That's," yawn, "great, Spook." He yawned again before falling fast asleep.

"Darned relaxing spray," said Spook, shaking his head. "Sends him to sleep every time he uses it. Better climb into bed yourself Toby. Once word gets out that the house is safe again, it will be crawling with Jeepers Creepers in no time. And they are always extra frightening after a break."

"Excellent!" said Toby, hopping back into bed.

"Just make sure you keep that Batbat out of sight. He may not look scary to you but . . . " Spook gave a shudder.

"I will," said Toby, putting Batbat deep under the covers. "Spook, could you do me a favor before you go?"

"Perhaps."

"Could you make sure Olivia hasn't gone to sleep yet, and that the Jeepers Creepers visit her room as well? I wouldn't want her to miss out," he smiled.

"I'd be delighted," said Spook. "Though," he gave a beastly chuckle, "I'm quite sure she's wide awake in her room right now, you know, just waiting . . . "

Glossary

ban
not allowed

darted
moved quickly

eternity
forever

lurk
move secretly

mohawk
haircut style where all hair but a strip in the middle of the head is shaved off

resolved
worked out

scared out of his wits
very frightened

soaring
very tall

sporting
having or wearing something

wheezing
breathing noisily

Looking at a Narrative

Introduction
(Who? What? Where?)

Who?
Toby, Olivia

What?
Olivia dares Toby to spend the night in the back room of Grandma's house.

Where?
At Grandma's house

Problem
(What happens? What goes wrong? How does the character feel?)

PROBLEM 1
Olivia scares Toby with stories about the Jeepers Creepers and how they will get him during the night. Toby is frightened by the strange shadows he sees and the sounds he hears. He grabs his old stuffed animal, Batbat, for comfort.

PROBLEM 2

Gathering his courage, Toby looks under the bed and discovers Spook and Lurk, two creatures from the Night Beastie Security Patrol. They are looking for a Heebie Jeebie, a creature more ferocious than a Jeepers Creeper. Toby takes Spook to talk to Olivia since she knows all about night beasties.

Resolution

(How the problem is solved)

Lurk thinks that Batbat is the Heebie Jeebie. When Toby explains that Batbat is harmless, the house is cleared for a Jeepers Creepers visit. This time, Toby is ready and he asks Spook to make sure that the Jeepers Creepers visit Olivia, too.

Comparisons to look out for

best	*silliest*	*stranger*	*bravest*	*more comfortable*
bigger	*furthest*	*darkest*	*closer*	*more excited*
slightest	*braver*	*wider*	*paler*	*deeper*

Pronouns to look out for

you	*she*	*he*	*I*	*it*
they	*his*	*your*	*my*	*them*
him	*her*	*me*	*we*	*us*

Author Lisa Thompson

Sometimes when I have guests stay over, they wake in the middle of the night after hearing strange noises. I can tell by the scared looks in their eyes they are thinking "Oh no! Not the Jeepers Creepers!" So I tell them it's just squirrels on the roof. But how would I know? I sleep with the light on!

Illustrator Mike Golding